TEN OF THE BEST MYTHS,
LEGENDS & FOLK STORIES

TEN OF THE BEST
GIANT STORIES

DAVID WEST

🏛 Crabtree Publishing Company
www.crabtreebooks.com

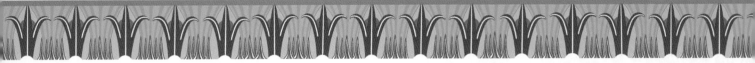

Crabtree Publishing Company
www.crabtreebooks.com
1-800-387-7650

Publishing in Canada
616 Welland Ave.
St. Catharines, ON
L2M 5V6

Published in the United States
PMB 59051, 350 Fifth Ave.
59th Floor,
New York, NY

Published in **2015 by CRABTREE PUBLISHING COMPANY.**
All rights reserved. No part of this publication may be reproduced,
stored in a retrieval system or be transmitted in any form or by
any means, electronic, mechanical, photocopying, recording, or
otherwise, without the prior written permission of copyright owner.

Printed in the U.S.A./092014/JA20140811

Copyright © **2014 David West Children's Books**

Created and produced by:
David West Children's Books

Project development, design, and concept:
David West Children's Books

Author and designer: David West

Illustrator: David West

Contributing Editor: Steve Parker

Editor: Kathy Middleton

Proofreader: Wendy Scavuzzo

Production coordinator and Prepress technicians:
Samara Parent, Margaret Amy Salter

Print coordinator: Katherine Berti

Library and Archives Canada Cataloguing in Publication

West, David, 1956-, author
  Ten of the best giant stories / David West.

(Ten of the best : myths, legends & folk stories)
Includes index.
Issued in print and electronic formats.
ISBN 978-0-7787-0824-7 (bound).--ISBN 978-0-7787-0821-6 (pbk.).--
ISBN 978-1-4271-7742-1 (pdf).--ISBN 978-1-4271-7734-6 (html)

  1. Tales. I. Title. II. Title: Giant stories.

PZ8.1.W37Gi 2014   j398.21   C2014-903852-6
                                           C2014-903853-4

Library of Congress Cataloging-in-Publication Data

West, David, 1956-
  Ten of the best giant stories / David West.
    pages cm. -- (Ten of the best: Myths, legends & folk stories)
  Includes index.
   ISBN 978-0-7787-0824-7 (reinforced library binding) --
  ISBN 978-0-7787-0821-6 (pbk.) --
  ISBN 978-1-4271-7742-1 (electronic pdf) --
  ISBN 978-1-4271-7734-6 (electronic html)
  1. Giants--Juvenile literature. 2. Mythology--Juvenile literature. I.
Title.

  GR560.W48 2014
  398.21--dc23
                                    2014022860

THE STORIES

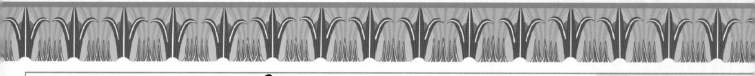

Cabracan

Cabracan was a Mayan giant who destroyed mountains. This is the story of how the hero twins, Hunahpu and Xbalanque, defeated Cabracan.

C abracan the giant was going about his business as usual—shaking the land and destroying mountains. Quaking the Earth made him feel good and he boasted about his greatness. This annoyed the gods and so they asked the twins, Hunahpu and Xbalanque, to put an end to the giant's boastfulness.

The two brothers set off in the direction of the trembling and quaking. They soon found Cabracan.

"Where are you going, great shaker?" they asked him.

"Nowhere," he answered. "I am staying to shake these mountains to the ground. Why are you here?"

Blowguns are long tubes that hunters blow poisonous darts from. Mayans used them to hunt animals.

"We are hunters," they replied. "We are on our way to a huge mountain where the Sun rises. There are many birds that we can shoot with blowguns."

"A huge mountain, you say?" said Cabracan, interested. "Take me there and I will shake it to the ground!"

The brothers agreed and all three set off toward the rising Sun. As they traveled, the twins kept a sharp lookout for birds to shoot and eat. At midday, they stopped to cook two birds they had killed. The smell of the birds roasting over a fire made Cabracan hungry.

"What is that you are cooking?" he inquired. "It smells good. Give me a piece to taste." The twins gave the giant one of the birds. They had already put poison on it. After the meal, they set off again.

Soon Cabracan fell to his knees. The brothers pounced on him, tied his hands and legs, dug a huge pit, pushed the giant into it, and buried him alive!

Today, earthquakes are much rarer. They happen when Cabracan struggles to free himself from his living grave deep in the earth.

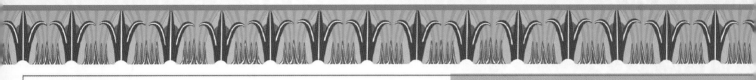

Ferragut

*Ferragut was a Saracen, or **Muslim**, warrior of enormous size. A descendent of Goliath (see page 12), his thick skin could not be cut by any blade.*

The giant named Ferragut had been sent to Spain by the **Emir** of Babylon to fight the **Christian** army of King Charlemagne. Ferragut feared neither dagger, sword, nor lance, and he had the strength of forty men.

Charlemagne, the king of the **Franks**, sent several of his champions to fight the giant. But Ferragut defeated all of them easily. Eventually, the hero named Roland met with the giant to do battle.

*"Saracens" was the name used for Muslims in Europe during the **medieval** era. Many battles were fought between Christian armies and Muslim armies during that time.*

For two days, the hero and the giant fought each other. But Roland could not find a way of wounding his foe. At night, the two stopped fighting to rest. But Ferragut had difficulty sleeping since he had no pillow upon which to rest his head. So, on the second night, Roland found a smooth, flat rock and kindly placed it under the sleeping giant's head.

The next morning, Ferragut was very taken with Roland's courteous behavior. He engaged him in conversation as they ate their breakfast. It was during this talk that the giant, by accident, mentioned his weak spot. "I am **invulnerable** to sword and arrow—except in my navel," he revealed.

It was Ferragut's undoing. As they resumed combat, Roland dealt a blow to the giant's navel and he fell to the ground, dead.

Roland was killed at the Battle of Roncesvalles, fighting against the Saracens. He blew his horn three times before Charlemagne heard it and rushed to his rescue with the main army. But it was too late—Roland had died.

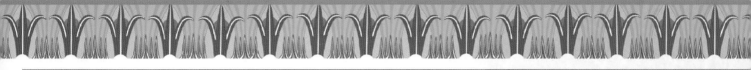

Finn McCool

*Finn McCool was a giant warrior in the mythologies of many **Gaelic** countries such as Ireland and Scotland. "Finn" is also a nickname, meaning fair or light-haired. McCool is sometimes described as having white hair.*

One day, as Finn was going about his regular business, a Scottish giant named Fingal began to shout insults at him across the Irish Sea. In anger, Finn lifted a lump of land and threw it at Fingal. It landed in the sea with a massive splash, creating the Isle of Man.

Fingal just laughed and hurled a few more insults at Finn. This made the Irish giant even more angry.

In his rage, he started throwing rocks into the sea to build a road, called a causeway, all the way to Scotland. It took him a week to finish. But, in the meantime, Fingal had grown bored. He wandered off to find someone else to insult.

Northern Ireland   Scotland

Ireland

Isle of Man   *Wales   England*

The Isle of Man is surrounded by the British Isles in the Irish Sea.

After finishing the causeway, Finn was very tired. Since there was no sign of Fingal, he returned home for a well-earned rest. He was just about to put his head on the pillow, when the ground began to tremble. It was Fingal crossing the causeway that Finn had just built!

"I am too tired to fight," said Finn to his wife. She replied, "Don't worry, dear. I have an idea." So she dressed him in baby clothes and put him in a large crib.

When Fingal arrived at Finn's house, Finn's wife welcomed him.

"My husband will be back soon. Will you not come in and wait?" she asked politely.

On entering the house, Fingal saw the massive crib with Finn lying in it. "What's in there?" he inquired.

"Oh, that's our baby, little Finn," replied the wife.

"My goodness!" thought Fingal, worried. "If that's his baby, how huge is Finn himself?"

Fingal quickly thought of a new plan. "I must be away **the noo**," he cried. "I have just remembered—I left the stove burning unattended!"

With that, Fingal ran back to his home in Scotland. On the way, he tore up the causeway behind him so that Finn could never follow.

The Giant's Causeway is a real place on the coast of Northern Ireland. It is made up of 40,000 six-sided columns of rock.

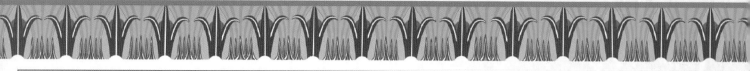

Geryon

Geryon was a monstrous giant of ancient Greek mythology who had three heads, six arms, and six legs. He owned a herd of magnificent red cattle.

Before the famous Greek hero Heracles could live forever, he had to complete twelve tasks, or labors, for King Eurystheus of Tiryns. His tenth task was to steal the cattle of the giant Geryon. This huge, fearsome warrior lived on the isle of Erytheia, far from King Eurystheus's court.

After traveling through a desert for many days, Heracles became angry at the heat and his lack of progress. In

frustration, he fired an arrow at Helios, the Sun god. Impressed with Heracles's courage, Helios allowed him to join him in his Golden Cup, which he rode across the sky daily from east to west. Thus, Heracles quickly arrived on the Erytheia shore.

*The watchdog, Orthrus, was the brother of Cerberus, the three-headed hell-hound that guarded the gates of the **Underworld**.*

Heracles was immediately attacked by the guardians of the cattle: the two-headed hound Orthrus and the herder Eurytion. With one huge blow from his olive-wood club, Heracles killed both the watchdog and the herder.

But as he gathered the cattle, the ground shook. In the distance appeared the towering shape of Geryon, moving toward him with enormous strides.

Heracles strung his bow and fired an arrow dipped in the poisonous blood of the Hydra, a serpent with many heads. The arrow struck Geryon in one of his foreheads. No one—not man, god, nor giant—could survive that terrible venom. Geryon crashed to the ground, stone dead. Heracles captured the cattle, completing his tenth labor.

Some of the cattle were later stolen by the fire-breathing giant Cacus. Heracles found him hiding in a cave with the animals, and clubbed him to death.

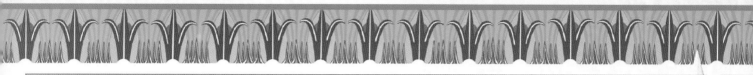

Goliath

*Goliath was a giant **Philistine** warrior whose story appears in the Bible.*

King Saul of Israel and his army faced the Philistine army near the Valley of Elah. The champion of the Philistines was the giant Goliath. For forty days, twice each day, he strode forward from his army lines to challenge the Israelites.

"Who will fight me to decide which side is the victor?" he called out.

Goliath was a mountain of a man, standing almost 10 feet (3 meters) tall. King Saul and the entire Israelite army were afraid.

A sling is an ancient weapon that serves to make the arm longer. It fires a stone like a bullet, at speeds of 100 feet (30 m) per second, over distances of 1300 feet (396 m).

A young boy named David arrived at the Israelite camp with food for his older brothers. When he heard that King Saul promised to reward any man who defeated Goliath, David accepted the challenge.

Saul could not believe that such a skinny boy could defeat a giant. He offered David his kingly armor but David declined, saying: "All I need is my sling." When Goliath saw David approaching he roared with laughter, as did the whole Philistine army. Goliath did not take the threat seriously—and this was his undoing. With one well-aimed shot, a pebble from David's sling hit Goliath in the forehead. The giant fell to the earth, lifeless.

Huge bugs have been named after this mythical giant. The Goliath beetle can reach 4.3 inches (11 cm) long and weigh up to 3.5 ounces (100 grams).

Kumbhakarna

In the Indian epic, called the Ramayana, Kumbhakarna —brother of Ravana—was a giant with a huge appetite.

The ground shook like an earthquake. Workers toiling in the fields looked around to see a monstrous giant rising from the earth. Dust and stones poured off him. It was Kumbhakarna, rising wearily from his six-month slumber.

The giant was hungry, and the people knew it. They ran in terror. Kumbhakarna snatched up and devoured the slowest. He would eat many of them before the day ended and he returned to his half-year sleep.

Saraswati is the Hindu goddess of knowledge, music, arts, and science. She possesses four arms, and is usually shown wearing a spotless white sari, or gown.

"How did Kumbhakarna get to this state?" you ask.

It was said that Kumbhakarna was so **pious**, intelligent, and brave that Indra, the leader of the gods, was jealous of him. When Kumbhakarna asked for a boon, or blessing, from Brahma, the god of creation, his tongue was cursed instead by the goddess Saraswati—acting on Indra's request.

So, when Kumbhakarna asked for what he really wanted, his cursed tongue instead requested that he go to sleep. His wish was granted. His brother Ravana asked Brahma to undo this boon, since it was really an evil spell. As a compromise, Brahma allowed Kumbhakarna to wake for one day every six months.

Ravana wanted help from his brother, Kumbhakarna, in his war against Rama. He drove 1,000 elephants over the slumbering giant to wake him up. Rama eventually won the battle.

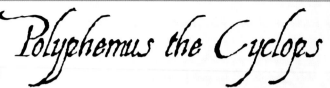 Polyphemus the Cyclops

In Greek mythology, the giant Polyphemus—son of the ocean-god Poseidon—was part of the one-eyed Cyclops clan.

On his journey home from Troy, Greek hero Odysseus landed on the island of the Cyclops to look for food and water. He and his men entered a cave where they discovered massive bowls and plates. Suddenly, huge sheep were herded into the cave—followed by a giant with one eye. It was a Cyclops. As the last sheep entered, the giant pushed a large boulder across to seal the entrance.

Odysseus emerged with his men from their hiding place.

"What is this? Strangers in my home!" shouted the Cyclops, tending his fire.

Odysseus bowed and, relying on the custom of hospitality, announced: "Our humblest apologies. We are travelers in search of **provisions**. I am Odysseus, and these are my men."

The Cyclops replied, "Pah! My name is Polyphemus, and I am hungry." Without warning, he grabbed two of the men and began to eat them!

Of the many one-eyed creatures in legends, the child from Japan called a Hitotsume-kozō is perhaps the strangest. It appears suddenly and surprises people—yet it is harmless.

In the morning, the Cyclops ate another two humans and left the cave with his sheep, pushing the boulder back across the entrance. That day, Odysseus made a plan and organized his men.

The next night, as the Cyclops lay sleeping, Odysseus and the other survivors drove a large wooden spike into Polyphemus's eye, blinding him. The Cyclops screamed in pain, but could not see to fight back. The next morning, as Polyphemus let out his sheep, he felt with his hands for anyone trying to escape by riding on top. The cunning Odysseus and his men did escape—by tying themselves to the undersides of the sheep.

As Odysseus sailed off with his men, he boastfully called out his own name. Not able to see, Polyphemus threw rocks toward the sound, narrowly missing the ship.

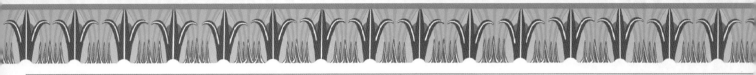

Sedna

*In **Inuit** mythology, Sedna is the goddess of the sea and marine animals.*

When the world began, there were giants. They lived on the land and ate the plants growing there. One day, a baby girl was born and her giant parents named her Sedna.

Each day, Sedna grew bigger. The larger she became, the more she ate. Eventually, she was greater in size than her parents. Soon there was not enough food—Sedna had eaten all the plants. The giants were becoming hungry.

The Inuit hunt seals in kayaks—small canoes made from animal skins wrapped around a wooden frame.

One night, Sedna's parents woke up screaming. She was trying to eat their legs! It was the last straw. They carried Sedna out to sea in their kayak and dropped her in the icy ocean. But when they tried to paddle back to land, the kayak would not move. Sedna was hanging on, and the kayak was in danger of tipping over.

"We will both drown if we do not do something!" wailed Sedna's mother. The father took out his knife and started to cut off his daughter's fingers. As the fingers fell into the sea, they turned into swimming creatures. One was a whale, another a seal. The fingers became all the animals of the sea.

With her fingers gone, Sedna sank to the bottom of the ocean. There the animals built her a home. She now lives in a deep, wintry, watery world, where ice forms a crust far above on top of the water.

Whenever the Inuit are short of food, they call on Sedna—and she provides it.

In 2003, a new space object was discovered beyond the farthest planet, Neptune. It was a dwarf planet. This red, icy world was named Sedna after the Inuit goddess.

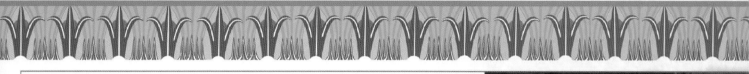

Skrymir

Skrymir was one of the giants—called Jotunns—of Norse mythology. He lived in the land of the giants, Jotunheim, in Castle Utgard.

One day the giant-bashing god Thor and the trickster-god Loki found themselves in Castle Utgard. The giant Skrymir had lured them by trickery, and they stood surrounded by giants in the great hall.

"Now that you two gods are here," said Skrymir, "you must entertain us with feats of strength."

Loki went first, but he lost an eating contest with the giant Logi. Next Skrymir turned to Thor.

"Perhaps a drinking contest?" he asked. A drinking horn was brought forward. "A good drinker could down this in one gulp!" claimed Skrymir.

Thor had a magic hammer and belt that doubled his strength.

Thor gulped and gulped, but the amount of drink hardly changed at all.

Skrymir smiled. "Pah! Not such a big drinker after all. Why not try to lift this large cat off the ground?"

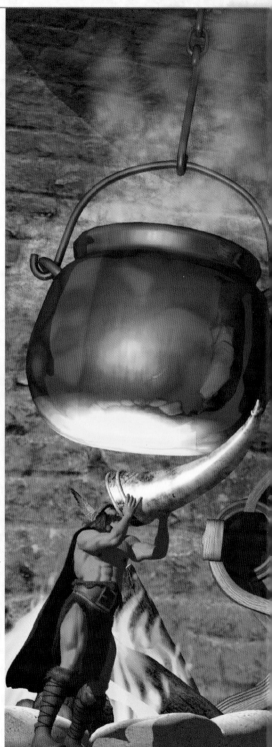

Thor could barely lift one paw of the cat from the ground. He gave up exhausted, but he was in a rage.

"I can defeat any of you in a fight!" he shouted.

Skrymir laughed and suggested he fight an old woman, who stood in a position ready to wrestle. Thor grabbed her and tried to throw her, but again he had no effect. Skrymir brought the contest to an end and allowed the two gods to sleep. The next morning, Skrymir took Thor and Loki to the edge of Jotunheim. Thor was miserable. How could he face the other gods? Skrymir took pity on him and let them in on his secret.

"We giants had heard of your strength, so we were unwilling to pit ourselves against you. The drinking horn was attached to the ocean. You actually lowered the level of the sea. The cat was really the Midgard serpent, which is so big it circles the Earth. Finally, the woman was old age. And no one can defeat old age."

In Norse mythology there will be a great battle, called Ragnarok, between the gods and the giants. It will signal the end of the world. Then a new Earth will be created.

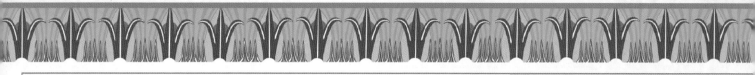

Talos

Talos was a bronze giant forged by Hephaestus, the Greek god of blacksmiths, for Zeus, the chief god. Talos was sent by Zeus to guard Europa, a Phoenician princess, who lived on the island of Crete.

Jason and his Argonauts were on their way back to Iolcus after a successful quest to capture the Golden Fleece for King Pelias. With them was the sorceress, or witch, Medea, who had used magic to help Jason with his quest. It had been a long and dangerous journey. Jason decided to stop at the island of Crete to take food and water onboard their ship, Argo.

As they approached the island they heard a screeching, as if metal was rubbing against metal. It quickly became louder. From behind a hill, a towering figure of rusting bronze suddenly appeared.

The myth of the Golden Fleece may have come from a type of early gold panning. Sheep fleeces, stretched over a wood frame, were submerged in a stream. Gold flecks floating past would collect in the wool. The fleeces were then hung in trees to dry, before the gold was shaken or combed out.

The figure was Talos, who began hurling rocks at the ship. Jason and some of the Argonauts leaped from Argo and raced up the beach toward Talos. Others began to row the ship away from the shore.

As Medea looked on, she realized that Jason and his men were in grave danger. Summoning her magical powers, she uttered a curse upon the advancing Talos. Suddenly the giant twisted, shook, and began grabbing at his ankle, where a nail stuck out. He ripped it away—releasing a cascade of hot, molten metal from within.

In seconds, the bronze giant crumpled to the ground, still and lifeless.

The Argonauts were named after their ship, Argo. The ship was named for its builder, Argus.

GLOSSARY

Christian A follower of the teachings of Jesus Christ

Emir A title for Muslim rulers

Franks A Germanic people that ruled western Europe in the Middle Ages

Gaelic Describing an ethnic group mainly in Ireland and Scotland

Inuit Indigenous people of the Arctic

invulnerable Not able to be injured

medieval The period of European history from the 5th to 15th centuries

Muslim A follower of the Islamic religion

Philistines An ancient people who lived in what is now southern Palestine

pious Devoted to God or gods

provisions Materials and supplies

the noo A Scottish phrase meaning "just now"

Underworld In mythology, a place where the dead dwell

INDEX